MADNESS

ARMAND CHARPENTIER (1864-1949), was a pacifist journalist who, around the end of the nineteenth century and the beginning of the twentieth, contributed Decadent and Naturalist fiction to the French press. His books include *Une Courtisane* (1893), *Le Roman d'un singe* (1895), and *L'Initiateur* (1897).

SHAWN GARRETT is a freelance editor, critic and short fiction aficionado. He currently co-edits the horror fiction podcast *Pseudopod* and posts weekly columns with *Rue Morgue*. His translations include Robert Scheffer's *Prince Narcissus and Other Stories* (Snuggly Books, 2019), and Gabriel Mourey's *Monada* (Snuggly Books, 2021).

ARMAND CHARPENTIER

CLAUSTROPHOBIC MADNESS

and Other Tales of Death and Love

transated by
SHAWN GARRETT

THIS IS A SNUGGLY BOOK

ISBN: 978-1-64525-119-4

The Translator dedicates this book to his sister, Lisa Ann Paradise, who has committed herself to one of the most honorable jobs left in our world—that of teacher of the young, as well as raising two wonderful children. I hope she finds the peace and satisfaction she desires.

CONTENTS

CLAUSTROPHOBIC MADNESS

CLAUSTROPHOBIC MADNESS

(Confession of a Suicide)

(originally published as "La folie claustropho-
bique (Confession d'un suicidé)" in *Revue des
journaux et des livres*, June 28 and July 5, 1896)

For Dr. Léon Puech-Legoyt

I

THE older I get, the more I feel this
... Terror growing in myself. After having been an intermittent nightmare all of my life, it has now become an obsession that lurks in my thoughts, monopolizes them, becomes a brain cancer which, day by day, expands its destructive work. I try to resist, but I fight in vain, as the Terror is stronger, my reason wavers and madness is near.

And what madness ... dear God, the worst of all! There are sweet delusions (I might almost call them a happy madness) that I will never take pity on: like the one in which, after a lamentable existence and following a mysterious break in his mind, one is persuaded that a crowd that acclaims him to be the New Messiah, or the one in which he governs innumerable people and has more diamonds and gold ingots than can be contained in the caves of his palace.

Certainly, someone who really believes something like that wouldn't want to be pitied. Withdrawn from the gloomy realities of existence, he lives in a perpetual dream, his eyes dazzled by the magnificent scenery that his fertile imagination creates and renews at any moment.

To want to cure such illnesses seems to me as inhuman as to awaken a sleeper whose smiling face reveals the voluptuous bliss of his dreams.

But my madness is much different! . . . I imagine it easily, knowing the cause from which it would come . . . what am I saying, it suffices for me just to think of it in order to suffer the frightful tortures. Yes, I can see myself in the dark of the tomb, suddenly waking from sluggish sleep, limbs bruised by the pressing planks, mouth and eyes filled with sawdust, unable to move, screaming with the full force of lungs already lacking sufficient air. And, knowing that no one would come, that a wall of earth separates me forever from the living, and thus waiting in minutes that will last for centuries, the most terrible of deaths.

And this triple sensation of asphyxia, of darkness, of being bound, these sensations which have become the theme of my madness would be the perpetual nightmarish end to my life, unless some problematic cure removes it from me. And so, rather than suffer this unimaginable torture for, perhaps years, I prefer to resort to immediate deliverance. That is to say, suicide.

Formerly, when the Terror assailed me, I struggled advantageously against its frights, believing that my youth and my health would preserve me from an approaching demise. Reasoning sensibly, I even realized that no symptoms of lethargic numbness had yet manifested, and it was puerile to live in fear of being buried alive while healthy.

But now that I'm nearing extreme old age, I have no more recourse to self-subterfuge in calming my fears. On the contrary, the closer I approach to the grave, the more the fear of waking in its icy solitude fixates in my thoughts at all times, becoming a perpetual obsession.

No doubt, I can inform my doctor that following my death I demand from him a careful examination of my corpse and, for greater certainty, that a pin be pushed not only into the soles of my feet but also into the region of my heart. In order to give weight to these last wishes, I can specify them in my will. Unfortunately, however good these precautions may be they are not enough to re-assure me. It may happen that the doctor forgets my recommendations, and that the will is opened after I am buried, and science will always be fallible, with even its most skilful practitioners prone to lethargy. I even believe that while suffering an *appearance* of death, the immobilized being is rendered immune to wounds which, at other times, would be mortal.

I have also thought about cremation. I owe much gratitude to the men of progress who, triumphing over ridiculous and dangerous prejudices, have succeeded in establishing crematoria in Paris. I have learned with joy that, in certain cases, this service is gratuitous and that the poor devils who are subject to a Terror analogous to mine have had the consolation of escaping the torments that they dreaded.

In the first sentence of my will I express my formal desire to be cremated. However, I will admit, the certainty of knowing that my flesh, my bones, my nerves, my muscles, everything which constitutes the whole of my body will be reduced to impalpable ash, only partially reassures me.

Here is why: more than twenty-four hours will pass between the moment when I am packaged in a temporary coffin and the time when the purifying flame will restore to impassible Nature the aggregate of materials of which I am made.

And what if, during this time, I woke up? . . . Who would hear my cries? . . . What helpful hands might unscrew the planks under which I smother? . . . Not wanting any minister of religion to watch over my agonies, and on the other hand having voluntarily deprived myself of any surviving family by confining my life to celibacy, I am not unaware that my bier would remain solitary, as well as the misshapen stool in front of the bed where I would lie dead. In itself, this abandonment does not displease me. Having always lived away from my contemporaries, whose harmful prejudices have so often afflicted me, my corpse has no need of their pity.

But it is the isolation of waiting that scares me. Ah! If it were possible for me to be carried directly from my sheets to the glowing hearth of the furnace, how lessened my Terror would be! And yet it would not entirely disappear, for if cataleptic lethargy petrifies the body, the mind still has all its lucidity. We are aware of what is said, of what is happening around us: we are witnessing our own burial.

How terribly, tortuously frightening it would be, that brief moment when one is lifted from the bed and gently squeezed between the walls of the coffin! What desperate movements would the arms be restricted from making, while a cry of a superhuman anxiety, rising from the depths of the soul, aborts in the paralyzed throat? And then, when darkness falls, when the ear perceives the first screws creaking in the oak, when one is irretrievably cut off from the living, to what infinite tortures will the mind be exposed, waiting for the alarm to sound?

Certainly, my suffering should be less, since I would know that in a few hours the flame would reduce me to nothingness. Nevertheless, I would then also anticipate the sensation of burning and the sound of the stove latch opening would resound lugubriously in my being.

However appalling these last moments may be, even disregarding cremation and imagining things at their worst, they would not last more than twenty-four hours, as by then asphyxiation would have come as an expected liberator, putting an end to my torture. Meanwhile, contrarily, my madness could last for months or years and during an endless succession of days I would see myself buried alive again and again, and I would have to repeatedly live through this imaginary night in the grave, a night of continual suffocation wherein I tormented my muscles with prodigious efforts to lift the unreal lid that pressed on my forehead. No! This claustrophobic madness, by which I am inevitably threatened, terrifies me far too much. I prefer to resort to suicide. By carefully pressing the tip of the revolver to my temple, there is a good chance that death will be almost immediate. However, this does not prevent me from specifying, for the sake of precaution, my formal desire to be cremated.

So, I have to kill myself. And tonight, I will.

II

AH! It is not without regret that I voluntarily condemn myself to death. Except for a few hours, here and there—hours of moral or physical suffering—life was kind to me.

Twenty years ago, even ten years ago, I never thought of dying voluntarily. But old age is a sad thing. Feeling your strength diminishing from day to day, seeing others around you constantly growing while monopolizing the same world which they drive you away from, parsimoniously measuring all the joy of your senses through a fear of illness and arriving at a hatred for the beauty, the youth, and the health of others because you are ugly, old and sickly. Such are the miserable lapses which I gradually sink into.

In spite of all this I would still yearn for life if this claustrophobic madness did not threaten me, for the elderly also gain consolations which are doubtless small but charming because of their very rarity. Yes, sometimes there are delicious hours of drunken excitement that can be conjured quite frequently with a little skill. The other week, I experienced some of them.

I was at the edge of the sea in a corner of deserted, almost wild, nature. A sky of a luminous blue, which the golden reflections of the sun traversed in all directions, extended to infinity, and behind the perceptible line of the horizon other spaces, luminous and vibrant with the sun, glowed. The waters seemed motionless, shimmering beneath the shower of light, and they brought with them a harsh rhythmic song which sounded against the rocks of the shore, as well as an echo in the inaccessible distance from which they came. And I was happy, truly happy beyond any expression. The magnificence of this vista filled me with the soul of immensity, the beneficent heat softened my limbs and lent them a false vigor, giving to my whole being a momentary, illusory return of youth. I think that if there had been a beautiful girl near me I would have loved her, as I had known love at thirty, and died in that, and the death would have been infinitely sweet to me. But loneliness surrounded me on all sides and my only consolation was to relive the past, to evoke the memories lived.

Had I loved the women of my past enough? Yes, I leave this world with the confidence of having adored them as much as human forces permit. I equally loved the women of the many different countries my vagabond nostalgia had exiled me to. I have loved blondes, brunettes and redheads, those with locks of black, copper and white; the small and the big; large ones with heavy chests and skinny ones; very young maids and nearly old women with gray hair; heavy peasants, badly clothed and naïve, and cleverly perverse socialites with slender limbs; high-priced courtesans and virgins who offered themselves for pleasure. I had loved them all and many others, all pursued by my desire, at all times and in all places.

But now that is all over. I am too old, love is forbidden to me. I do not wish any longer to arouse useless suffering with the aphrodisiacs of the past. I prefer to go to my death in all serenity, without superfluous regrets. And I want to use my last hours to finish this confession of a claustrophobic, to show the slow, gradual growth of this madness in my brain.

III

AS far as my memory reveals, it was in the distant years of my youth when I felt the first symptoms of this strange malady. I had, innate in me, a fear of darkness and an anguish of being confined. As a child, playing with comrades of my age, it was hard for me to hide in a dark cabinet, not for fear of some fabulous animal or a bloodthirsty robber like so many other children, but simply because I felt a choking sensation and it always seemed as if the air was running out. And the darkness added to my terror in the sense that by not seeing the walls I imagined them very close, and my discomfort at being restrained increased all the more.

At the coming of winter there occurred a singular day of the illness, that being the day chimneys were swept. In the silence of the motionless streets of the province, I could hear from afar the cry of the poor boy who, besides a boss whose appearance was somewhat barbaric to my eyes, trotted on his short, soot-blackened legs.

I could not avow that this child worked voluntarily for this man, and it was quite possible he had been stolen when very young, then deprived of food and beaten until he agreed to do this horrible job.

The pity I felt on seeing him kneel in front of chimneys, passing his skinny body through the opening of the trapdoor and disappearing into the big black hole, those pitiful emotions which tightly hugged my heart were certainly the first feelings of my young existence.

To make matters worse, the ugly master always wanted to close the hatch, so that the falling soot did not dirty the floor as he waited quietly with us. I wanted to stop him from being so cruel but his fierce looks frightened me, and then I also saw that my parents approved of his action, probably fearing for the furniture. So I was silent, waiting anxiously for the return of the little chimney sweep.

My God, how long the five or six minutes of his absence seemed to me! . . . "What if

he could not come down again?" I thought
. . . and I suffered alongside him, imagina-
tively putting myself in his place, locked in
that dark pipe between four narrow walls,
suffocating and unable to call anyone, knowing all help was impossible. How would I
withdraw from there, if I were suffocating?
. . . A thousand chimerical fears haunted my
child's weak brain, until the moment I saw
him reappear, bent in two, taking out his
legs first, then the shoulders and finally his
blackened head, illuminated by the smile of
his calm and resigned eyes.

When he had gone up all our chimneys,
my mother gave him two *sous*, while the
barbarian man, who was not fatigued (having done no work), received a *pièce blanche*,
which seemed unfair to me. I hardly had the
notion of money then, and I did not know
how indispensable it was for living, did not
suspect all the good things that it procured.
Despite this, an imprecise rebellion dawned
on me regarding this unequal distribution of
wages and I regretted that I was not rich, that
I did not have two penny coins in my pocket
or piggy bank, because I would have slipped
them into the hand of the little chimney
sweep with pleasure.

If he went away without my money, at least he carried away all the tenderness of my dreaming soul in the misery of his black rags, and for all of my youth and even later, well after I was a man, his memory was the reminder of emotions both painful and charming.

I would not dare to say that in acclimating me to sleeping with a night light, my mother had involuntarily helped midwife that curious mental illness which modern science calls claustrophobia, as that would probably be an exaggeration. But it is quite certain that her maternal precaution may have developed those latent seeds of evil, instead of destroying them.

As a young man, when I desired to reject this habit, it was already too late. My will was impotent and, in order not to suffer each evening from the same eternal nightmare that even today leads me to suicide, I had to resign myself to keeping a light in my room, despite the silliness of this childish mania.

It was not that light was necessary to me for actual sleep, but because every time I awoke and open my eyes in the middle of the night, in that tenth of a second of the awakening, a powerful nightmare began in which I lost my sense of place, horrible enough in fact that I uttered frightful screams.

I imagined I was in my grave, all the air was gone from my lungs, the bedsheets were the winding shroud wrapped around me as I choked and screamed desperately, calling for help, feeling more and more asphyxiated, until I saw a ray of light or heard a human voice. I had that sudden dream of being buried alive hundreds and hundreds of times.

Many times when I went to bed in the evening, during the minutes just preceding sleep, I had the desperate thought that I would fall asleep forever, remain in lethargy long enough to be believed dead, only to awake in the leaden sheath of the tomb! Despite my best efforts to drive it away, that thought returned to haunt me and today it has become an obsession. In addition to this anticipated martyrdom was the suffering at the thought of departing life suddenly, in full health, with plans unrealized, friends to see again, a mistress to love, women to desire.

I had, in all forms, a fear of confinement. The sight of a trunk, a wardrobe, immediately suggested to me the thought of being shut up inside, while my too fertile imagination presented visions of desperate efforts to struggle against walls in painful tension, attempting to escape suffocation.

A similar fear paralyzed me in cellars and in tunnels. I thought of the sudden collapse of the mass of stone overhead and saw myself buried under the rubble, surrounded by the jumble of beams and materials, deprived of light, suffocating, gasping, making super-human but useless efforts to escape the slow agony of asphyxiation I knew would come. With what anxious attention would my ear listen for the pickaxe which brings a breath of air, while one feels the formidable weight of a mountain of earth and stones on his broken limbs!

I have experienced all these tortures so of-ten that I know them as if I had really suffered them, and they would bring no new pain to me. My brain has been steady enough to re-sist this perpetual obsession for many years. I am not a writer but if I were, mere words or sentences could not capture and express these exact qualms. Perhaps some patients may read these pages and gain an approximate idea of my continual torture, just like ether itself proves powerless to provide them with artificial respiration.

If I had lived in the Middle Ages, those times when the life of man counted so little, justice depended on the good pleasure of a few and punishments were simply refined barbarism, my great fear might have been that some mighty enemy would immure me alive, or that an intolerant priest would attempt to subdue my rebellious spirit by the solitude of a dungeon cell.

Moreover, in spite of feeble liberties won from the tumble of revolutions, the punishment of claustration still exists in our laws. I will always remember the impression of terror that I received, many years ago, when on board a ship I saw the cell in which seamen were imprisoned for twelve, and sometimes twenty-four, hours. Whatever the faults of these men, that atonement is far too terrible. I had to turn away, my anguish suffocating me as I stood before this square hole with a ceiling too low to stand upright, which was closed with a heavy iron door pierced with a dormer, for letting in a few breaths of air. If I were locked in such a cage, it is certain that I would die there. But, when my corpse was removed, no one would ever know what inexpressible tortures were a prelude to my agony . . .

IV

HOWEVER imperfect the feeling of terror that I have tried to record, if anyone should read these pages one day, he will hopefully understand the half-nervous and half-cerebral disease from which I have suffered. He will easily imagine the gradual increase of my claustrophobic fear from its first manifestations until the day when it became an obsession. And now that this obsession more tenaciously leads me to madness day by day, he might perhaps find it natural that, although able to live a few years happy and without infirmities, nevertheless I do not hesitate to commit suicide to free myself from this cabinet called life.

I die regretting my life, but with no fear of my Death. I die with the consciousness of having done very little harm to my fellow men. I have always striven to be good and just to others, mastering as far as possible jealousy, antipathies, hateful appetites, all those instincts of primitive man that our ancestors have given us.

Certainly, I know nothing of where I am headed. Perhaps it is simply an ultimate annihilation, the absolute cessation of life, the scattering of matter, the definitive disappearance of the ego. In that case, no suffering is to be feared, no joy to be hoped for. The return to nothingness does not frighten me. As dust mingled with the dust of dead generations, I will thus be a few atoms of the fertile soil from which will spring the nourishing harvests of the future.

And perhaps Death is also an awakening, a deliverance? Just as blood runs under our flesh, it is possible that an invisible fluid envelops us on all sides, forming under our physical skin an immaterial one, drawing a fluidic silhouette, in a word, analogous in form, movement, and resemblance to our body. This intangible being, this *astral body*, is none other than our soul, that is to say, the thought we carry in ourselves, the thought which moves our muscles by means of some mysterious triggering, which lights in our eyes a flame alternately brilliant or agonizing.

The thought which allowed us to invent the Arts and Sciences to combat our boredom, the thought which suggests Love to us, with all its joys, its pleasures, its delusions. The thought, finally, that is the initial creator, the source of life.

Death would then be the great liberator, coming to deliver our *self* from the animal skin that imprisons us. When the act is consummated, when the bonds are broken, the soul regains its liberty and, being imponderable, it must have the gift of speed and therefore the possibility of crossing immeasurable space in the fragments of a second.

And it must be delicious to glide in the infinite, really, to travel from globe to globe, to be no more than a living form, crossing at will the celestial immensities.

This vision is attractive to me. I want to know what lies beyond the tomb. Another five minutes, and I will summon Death to me . . .

Farewell, O World. I leave life with serenity.

THE FUNERAL
SUBSCRIPTION

(originally published as "L'Abonnement
Funeraire" in *Le Bambou: périodique illustré* of
1893)

I

"HEY! Eh!" thought M. Coffignon "for almost three hours I have been seventy . . . a good age, damn! . . . and still solid at the post!"

Although he tried to joke with himself, an imperceptible sadness was pounding through him, rising from the unknown depths of his being, then becoming clearer with the awareness of approaching death. Because death would come terribly quickly, the one to whom we do not give ourselves but who takes you all the same, at the precise minute assigned for the meeting. Would it be tomorrow, in a week or a decade? He did not know. And his regret at life, the eternal despair of feeling powerless to go back, to take back the past few years, threw his soul into sudden melancholy.

However, this existence which he clung to so tenaciously had hardly been fruitful in pleasures. From an early age he had turned off "that which is the joy and reason for being." Selfishly withdrawn, his heart did not thrill at any emotion, his brain nourished no thought of another, his flesh did not quiver at anyone's touch. Dominated by the dirtiest, the most disgraceful and only inexcusable vice, avarice, he thought only of amassing gold, amassing it in secret without anyone suspecting it, so that everyone believed him to be poor and yet he alone knew himself to be rich. He had lived miserably, refusing not only the appearances of luxury but even the bare necessities. Keeping his family distant, with no friends and no women in his life, he spent his days earning as much as possible in the most extraordinary trades, buying here to resell there at a profit, however small it may have been. The certainty of gaining two sous would have made him cross all of Paris and, in the evenings, he would go to bed at nightfall, so as not to burn lights.

Favored by insolent luck, this man who had no need of money (since he preferred to live frugally rather than spend it) realized the most unforeseen gains, sniffed out the most advantageous opportunities, successfully operated the most daring investments. He had decided once by chance, though he never played, to buy a lottery ticket (at a discount). Three months later he won the jackpot of five hundred thousand francs. After sixty years of such an existence, he now found himself possessing several millions. Most of his fortune, hidden in banks, was still invested through overlapping interests, to continued increase. The rest slept at his home, in large, carefully sealed wardrobes. There, on the shelves, piles of gold, silver and copper alternated in perfect alignment, while in the lower shelf wads of blue banknotes were piled up and tied with white cords. And his great joy, his only joy, was to open the cupboards to add a handful of gold coins to the pile, to re-count the whole and to harmonize the piles.

Then, his flesh tingling, his heart dilating with happiness, he caressed his riches with a slow hand, sneering: "Eh, eh! . . . my siblings think me poor . . . miserable . . . and I am richer than all of them together! They will be surprised when I die!"

On reaching his seventies he had become more concerned with his own end, which he guessed was approaching, although the more or less continual fast to which he had become accustomed had kept his body in perfect shape and health. In itself, death did not frighten him, it was only his burial that worried him. By an inexplicable contradiction of spirit, after having lived so meagerly, he desired a grandiose funeral, a funeral whose princely luxury would dazzle the passers-by. He reveled in the idea of resting on a comfortable bier, under a high catafalque, adorned with immense draperies strewn with silver droplets, of going to church surrounded by the most pompous ceremony, of attending a mass which twelve priests would celebrate under the shimmer of five hundred candles, and then to proceed towards the cemetery in the most sumptuous of the carriages, covered by flowers and dragged by six caparisoned horses on whose heads would wave heavy black plumes.

Unfortunately, such a funeral would be expensive, and he remained stingy, even in death, unwilling to impose such an expense on his heirs. Several times he had visited various funeral directors to find out the exact prices. All of them gave analogous answers:

"For the funeral you want, that is to say a first-class affair . . . with mass sung, six horses, flowers, a catafalque . . . you're looking at fifteen thousand francs at the least . . ."

"Fifteen thousand francs!"

"Yes sir."

"But that's horribly expensive."

"You want it to be beautiful, don't you?"

"Everything at its most beautiful."

"So, you have to pay the price . . . You see, sir, in funeral pomp, as in everything, you only get what you pay for."

Fifteen thousand francs! The enormity of the figure astounded M. Coffignon. How could he spend more money in a few hours than he had in ten years?

No, such madness was not possible. And despite the intensity of his desire, he resisted specifying such a funeral in his will. It was a continual struggle between his frenzied greed and the tempting envy that plagued him, but the former always triumphed.

II

HE was trying to escape this temptation of posthumous luxury, transferring all of his thoughts to his gold, caressing it more often, absorbing himself in it, when one day he found, slipped under the door of his miserable home, the following leaflet:

PAILLARDOT HOUSE
FATHER AND SON AND INC.
FUNERAL POMP, CONVEYANCE
TRANSPORT, ETC.
Numerous Medals for Various Exhibitions
Phone

M.

The Maison Paillardot, Father and Sons and Inc., well-known to its numerous customers, has the honor to bring to your attention that it will inaugurate, from next July 1, an absolutely new funeral system through the Funeral Subscription.

However great the family affections, however sincere the pain of our loved ones, we must always reckon—alas!—with the ingratitude inherent in human nature. This is why many people, after death, do not get the funeral that they wanted during their lifetime. In order to remedy this state of affairs, the Paillardot Father and Son and Inc. company has just created the Funeral Subscription.

From now on, everyone can secure a funeral to their liking. For a monthly or quarterly payment, varying according to age and health, our customers have the option of subscribing to their own funerals and paying in advance, exactly the scheduling of their convoy, specifying the quantity of flowers they want, etcetera. In order to fully explain the multiple advantages of our system, we will cite one example among many: A man of forty, enjoying normal health and free from infirmities will be entitled, subject to a quarterly payment of forty-five francs, to a first-class funeral with an actual value of ten thousand francs, regardless of the time of death. Finally, we will add that our funeral subscriptions, duly specified and initialed on stamped paper, remain valid for all types of death: Crimes, Accidents or Suicides.

It is indisputable that those who are destined to become centenarians will lose in this market; on the other hand, those to which death—as cruel as it is premature—steals from the affection of their own will find real benefits. Funeral subscription, therefore, becomes in a way a lottery; so we have no doubts about its success, given the playful Gallic temperament which characterizes our race and has earned us for all time the reputation of being the most spiritual people in the universe.

In the hope that you will honor us with your trust, we inform you, M., that we will be giving our first 100 subscribers a 25% discount off regular rates.

Please accept, Sir, our respectful and eager greetings.

PAILLARDOT,
Father and Son and Inc.

"By Jove," murmured M. Coffignon, as soon as he had read the prospectus, "here is what suits my business . . . and I will, today, run to this M. Paillardot to benefit from the announced offer."

III

WITH the deal concluded, M. Coffignon was delighted. For a subscription of 50 francs per month, he had secured a magnificent first-class funeral, with catafalque, flowers and sung mass, with a real value of fifteen thousand francs. Although, it was not without haggling that he had managed to secure such an advantageous deal. Given his age, and following examination by the specialist doctor attached to the establishment, the Paillardot Father and Son and Inc. company only wanted to accept a monthly subscription of 100 francs. But he cried out: "One hundred francs . . . twelve hundred francs a year! . . . but it is horribly expensive . . . it is positively overpriced."

"But think, Sir, that you are over seventy . . . and moreover you choose for your burial all that is the most expensive!"

"Sir, my parents both died past 100 and I myself enjoy excellent health . . . never a cold . . . I can very well live another twenty years, so that I will have you paid twenty-four thousand francs . . . without counting the interest on the money!"

"Very well, sir, but if—which I do not wish—you die tomorrow . . . it will be a net loss of fifteen thousand francs for the house."

M. Coffignon argued for a long time. In the end, he won his case; and, as he was incredibly lucky to be the ninety-seventh customer, he took advantage of the advertised reduction, which reduced his subscription to 50 francs per month.

He returned home perky and carefully placed the precious treaty beside the stacks of gold and blue notes. In the evening he allowed himself half a bottle of good wine for his dinner as a sign of joy, an indulgence that he had only allowed himself two or three times in his life.

IV

FROM then on, M. Coffignon was the happiest man in the world. Had he not realized the dream of his life? His greatest pleasure was to meet a funeral in the street. He shrugged, pitying the poor devil who was going underground so miserably. Only the second and first class chariots, a little more frequent since the brilliant invention of the Paillardot House, Father and Sons and Inc., obtained his flattering approval. And yet, these funerals still seemed very petty to him compared to the one he would have. He imagined attending his own funeral and dreamed about it constantly, seeing the crowd of onlookers remove their hats as the hearse passed, all of them intrigued by the sumptuousness of the convoy. This was the favorite theme of his thoughts and he reveled in it.

Now he was no longer afraid of death; on the contrary he was almost anxious to enjoy the only luxury he had allowed himself – a posthumous luxury. There was nothing left for him to do down on earth. Undoubtedly he could still earn a few thousand francs, adding to the millions which were sleeping in his safes. But his fortune was large enough and he was delighted at the pleasant surprise he would give his siblings who thought him poor. And it was a joy that he was eager to taste—posthumously as well. He laughed in advance, with a little dry and nervous laugh, imagining the amazement of those close to him opening the wardrobes and seeing the tall piles of gold and silver, shining, immovable in their aligned columns . . .

. . . However, the years passed and M. Coffignon remained stronger than ever, going out in all weather, eating sparingly of un-delicate foods, refraining from wine, not patching his torn clothes. Never even a fainting spell, so that it seemed that death did not want him.

Already, in three years, he had paid 1,800 francs for a funeral subscription. Every month, he painfully pulled a 50-franc note from his drawers and carried it to the Paillardot Father and Sons and Inc. house. And each time it was a real heartbreak; he suffered as much as if he was witnessing the looting of his house. One morning he went to a free hospital consultation, hoping he would be discovered to be dangerously ill.

"How old are you?" asked the doctor after a careful auscultation.

"Seventy-three, sir."

"Well, my friend, you can go on like this for another thirty years . . . you are the wood from which are made centenarians . . ."

M. Coffignon returned home absolutely furious. If this doctor were telling the truth, if he was going to live another thirty years, why, thirty years in which every month he would have to pay his fifty francs would finally give a nice total of 19,800 francs! Thus, instead of having a first-class funeral for next to nothing, thanks to his membership, he would have paid them 4,800 francs too much! Ah, no, it just could not be! And in his fear of being the dupe in this finalized deal, in his haste to finally enjoy the only money he had spent in his life, in his desire above all to spend as little as possible for his funeral, he coldly decided to cut short his days.

. . . And, while a charcoal stove was burning in the middle of his room, he stretched out on his pallet, smiling at the coming death, once again reminding himself of the vision of the majestic chariot drawn by six horses and followed by the crown-bearers bending under the weight of the flowers, of the church hung in black, of the organs, and the altar glowing by the light of the candles and the twelve priests proclaiming liturgical hymns for his soul to rest.

"Hee! Hee!" He sneered with a last hiccup, "those good gentlemen, Paillardot Father and Sons and Inc!"

THE ASSASSIN-POET

(originally published as "Le poète assassin" in
Revue des journaux et des livres, January 3, 1886)

I

BY what circumstances had he happened to commit the crime? He did not know anything about it himself, and had certainly been the plaything of implacable fate.

The scene of the murder, in the crudity of its smallest details, continually haunted his memory. He saw the vile one again, standing before him with all the striking details of reality. Her long hair, with raven wing glints, was twisted at the top of her head and it emanated heavy, sleepy perfumes. Her eyes commanded forgiveness instead of merely imploring it, and her lips, accustomed to deceptive kisses, opened to utter fallacious oaths.

But he had killed her coldly, not wanting to see anything, to hear anything, with the certainty of an unforgivably foul misdeed.

His name was Rodolphe Planson and he was not yet twenty-five. After finishing his studies, he had given himself over entirely to the arts and already he had written a novel, and a drama which slept in a box, in truth, but which might any day make him famous, as the texts had a seal of originality which only the genius possesses, and which is sufficient for a work of talent to emerge from the crowd of books.

Admittedly, once on the benches of the Assize Court, he easily could have saved his head, although and even perhaps only receiving a weak conviction.

But seeing his future irretrievably lost, and tired of a life that until then seemed only an evil stepmother, he resolved to end it all . . . as an *original*. After all, he thought, *not to be*, to have *no sensations*, was less unpleasant than the alternate.

He began by refusing a lawyer and choosing to defend himself, as it was his idea to amuse himself at the expense of the world in general, and the expense of the judges in particular. The prison guards were astonished to hear him laugh, not the vague and continuous titter of the madmen, but that truly human guffaw of a man of sound reason.

But the jury and the public were even more surprised when he started, in court, with these words:

"Gentlemen judges, gentlemen of the jury, and you vain crowd who hang on my words, I begin by declaring to you that I will not seek in any way to defend my thinking, for that is what all the condemned do, and I have a horror of doing as others do . . ."

Here the president interrupted him:

"What are you going to do, then?"

"What am I going to do, Mr. Chairman? Oh, it's very simple! I'll give you something for which you can condemn me to death . . ."

A second interruption by the president:

"Accused, do you know that a lot is at stake in this game?"

"Mr. President, it seems to me that it is not up to you, being a Catholic and a married man, to use that term. For as a Catholic, you must know what eternal delights await us beyond life, beyond the grave, when a soul released from the bonds of matter glimpses the magical apotheoses of unknown paradises where loved ones, virgins, and exotic dancers come to offer themselves for holy, permitted luxuries. Lastly, as a married man, you are not unaware of the perpetual boredom which escort us, beyond the grave, when the body, freed from the bonds of clothing, approaches that of a bride which twenty-five years of marriage have made far too legitimate."

A third interruption by the president:

"Accused, I seriously remind you to stay prudent while retaining your seriousness."

"With prudence, do you say, Mr. President? Ah! I find the judge here is in what I will call, with or without your permission, the quintessence of imbecility. For you will agree with me, gentlemen, it is not for you to speak of prudishness when you or your predecessors had the impudence to prosecute *Madame Bovary* by Flaubert, or even more recently *La Chanson des Gueux* by Richepin, as an offense to morality."

A fourth interruption by the president:

"Accused, you avoid the subject that brings you to this place."

"If I avoid the question, it is because the question is too simple for me to linger over. It boils down to this: I killed my mistress. That is true. Not because she cheated on me, but because if I had let her live she would have been cheated on, sooner or later, by her new lover, whom she adored, and she would have committed suicide from the anguish. You see, gentlemen of the jury, that I have prevented her from killing herself, and that I have acted only out of pure charity, Christian or secular, whichever you wish.

✳

All of his arguments were of this tone. Some judges argued that he was crazy; but then he would become serious again and show the specialist doctors that he had his full reason.

He was sentenced to death.

Once in his cell at Roquette, he obtained paper, ink and quills "to pass the time" (as he said) during his last days of existence. They wanted him to sign a pardon, but he never consented to give his signature. He preferred to die.

His crime and sentencing had made a lot of noise in the newspapers. He had become the hero of the day. In the salons, they spoke only of "this original Rodolphe Planson." The journalists came to see him, reproducing in their rags the conversations they had with him. One day a *Figaro* reporter begged him to write something for the *literary supplement*.

"But a year ago I sent you an article every week, why didn't you print those?"

"Because then . . ."

". . . I was an honest man, and now I am a murderer?"

"No, because then you were unknown, ignored, while now your name is known to everyone."

"From which it follows that to acquire a prompt celebrity one must kill his fellow man."

"You exaggerate."

"No, it is the logical consequence of your words. Besides, I do not blame you. My eyes have seen enough of the spectacle of the world, it is time for me to turn and look on the other side. Come tomorrow, at this same time, and I'll give you a *novel* little piece for your supplement."

The piece appeared, and the paper sold ten times more copies.

Then the publishers came looking for him, they who had formerly deigned to receive him into the heights of their greatness and then had invariably dismissed him with mocking and impertinent smiles, such smiles as worn for the one who has nothing by the ones who have everything. These publishers arrived at La Roquette humble, obsequious, crawling like beggars, arguing with bank notes over the manuscripts of his novels.

He gave them all of it, including a volume of verse, but not without deliberately creating an unknowing spectacle more rare than a white blackbird or a member of the Salvation Army without a Bible: an unpublished novelist draining his publishers.

Some time later, a charitable society organized a concert for the poor. Rodolphe Planson wrote these few words to the organizer of the festival:

"Sir, do you want to make a big profit? If so, get the prefect's permission to list me among your artists. I think I have some talent and even more celebrity—good, bad or what have you!—that I am happy to put at your disposal, for the benefit of a noble charity."

The police gave permission. On the posters announcing the festival, before the names of the principal actors, was printed:

> . . . with the help of Rodolphe
> Planson, *The Assassin-Poet*

The tickets, which until then had not moved very much, sold out in a few days at triple the price with this advertisement.

Rodolphe Planson appeared twice on the program. In the first part he declaimed *La Conscience*, by Victor Hugo. The spectators could not help feeling a chill of terror cool their bones at hearing this man, whose head would be sliced off in a few days, hurling in a dark and powerful voice, from full lungs, that masterly verse:

The eye in the grave looked at Cain.

In the second half, dressed as the condemned man at the moment of execution, he recited his own poem *Before the Gallows*, which he intended to recite again on the platform of the guillotine at the supreme moment.

His success was immense: the whole room applauded and stamped with enthusiasm. Six months before they would never have even listened to him.

A few days before his execution, he received a visit from a professor of the *Faculté de médecine*, who asked if he was willing to lend himself to certain experiments.

"Monsieur," replied Rodolphe Planson, "I love science almost as much as the belles-lettres, which is to say not at all, but it is with real pleasure that I put my head and my body at your disposal. Do whatever you want."

"For the experiment that I have in mind, you would have to agree in advance."

"Tell me, then."

"I have obtained, not without difficulty and contrary to custom, a false burial for you. After the execution your body and your head will be immediately delivered to me. In order not to lose a minute, I will have all my devices near me, behind the gallows. Once your head has fallen into the basket, I will pick it up and put it in an automaton that I have made. Electrical wires will communicate with your nerves. You will try to speak and, if you succeed, you will tell me the *sensations* you feel. Do you understand?"

"Very well."

"And you consent?"

"Perfectly!"

"I thank you in the name of science and I will see you soon."

"See you soon!"

※

On the morning of his last day, Rodolphe Planson received a visit from a priest. "Sir," said the latter, "I come to hear your confession and bring you Holy Communion."

"Monsieur curé, thank you very much. Unfortunately, as I believe very firmly that any two bodies placed in space have attraction in direct proportion to their mass and in inverse proportion to the square of their distance, I do not believe at all in the immortality of the soul. So you will find that I will not touch the host."

The priest insisted for a few moments but, seeing that he was dealing with a profound skeptic, had the honesty to no longer speak of religion.

An hour later, Rodolphe Planson, calm and smiling, arrived at the foot of the guillotine. The professor of the *Faculté* asked him:

"Do you remember our deal, regarding the experiment?"

"Yes," Rodolphe replied, "do not be anxious."

Then, slowly dragging out the rhythm, he recited his poem *Before the Gallows*. Here are the first three stanzas:

*Guillotine, the only mistress who
does not deceive her lover,
I will soon feel your caress all over.*

*I will lay on the board,
Put my head through the hole,
So that your heavy knife takes its toll.*

*Be full of lust for me!
As my head very slowly
Rolls in the sawdust, lasciviously!*

The last stanza finished, he turned to the guillotine, stretched out all the way on the board without guidance from the hand of the executioner's valet, and then ran his head through the hole, shouting: "*Pull the . . .*"

That *last syllable* remained in his throat. His head rolled into the basket.

The doctor picked it up and placed the nerve endings, hanging like threads of frayed cloth, in communication with electric batteries. The face of the decapitated contracted horribly, the eyes rolled in their sockets, the eyelids closed and opened automatically.

"Can you talk?"

"Ye . . . s."

"What do you feel?"

"I . . . suf . . . fer . . . ve . . . ry much . . ."

That was all. The eyelids closed forever.

A gloomy silence enveloped the spectators of this scene, and only the electric bell that made the battery run continued its *ringing . . . ringing . . . ringing . . .*

✳

Ringing . . . Ringing . . . Ringing . . .

"Rodolphe, open up, it's me."

"Who?"

"Henriette, for goodness sake! You don't recognize my voice?"

Rodolphe Planson jumped out of bed, put on his trousers, and went to open his door.

"Ah! Where am I and who are you?"

"You dream while awake now? You are at home and I have come to see if you want to make peace or you are still angry from last night."

"So I'm not dead . . . the gallows . . . it was a horrible dream . . . my novel is not printed . . ."

"Are you crazy? What do you mean about the gallows?"

"Imagine, that I dreamed of having killed you . . . oh! But I must tell you . . ."

"Listen! It's splendid weather . . . if you want, we could lunch in the country . . . you'll tell me your dream on the grass . . ."

"I don't mind, but let's stop by La Roquette first, so that I can be assured that my gallows existed only in a dream."

THE ADVENTURE OF JACQUES PÉTROMÉ

(originally published as "L'Aventure de Jacques Pétromé" in *La Lanterne: journal politique quotidien*, October 28, 1905)

I

JACQUES Pétromé, thinking that he had spread enough sugar to his contemporaries (with or without melancholy, as the sweet poet would say), doubly resolved one day to sell his shop and live on the eight thousand francs income he had earned in twenty years of work.

Six months later our grocer, who until then had considered marriage as only for the insane, took for a legitimate wife Marguerite Grélin, whose father occupied a very beautiful position in the funeral business.

Two or three friends charitably warned him in vain that he was going to bury himself. Jacques did not listen to them, thinking, not without reason, that a wedding bed was, of all tombs, that one where life was most pleasantly enjoyed.

If one of the great statisticians (who honor the century in general, and the French administration in particular) had consulted individually, on the day following the marriage, the former female customers of the ex-grocer, they would have collected only words of praise.

All of the women would have stated that never, in the memories of both old concierges and young gavroches, did a grocer balance more elegantly the packets of candles and the boxes of sardines, formed more beautiful arabesques with fake and natural coffee, wrote his name in a more exquisite way among the melting sweets with the pink and white sugared almonds and, above all, sang the price of the goods more melodiously.

But had the same statistician gone, just afterwards, to the young wife of Jacques Pétromé he would have had to record bitter and violent criticisms of the new husband. Marguerite would have told him very clearly that never was a wreath of orange blossoms more foolishly, nor more heavily, stripped away.

I humbly admit to ignoring the conclusion that such an eminent and honorable statistician would draw from this praise and this criticism.

As for me, poor wretch, I will stupidly formulate this axiom: a great man gives unexpected and quite charming attention to old, salted fish in his shopfront, but he is still nothing more than a poor fool when he finds himself alone with his wife.

Now that I have spoken of Jacques Pétromé's marital disabilities, my readers will not be surprised if I tell them that, after six months of marriage, the unfortunate husband caught his wife in the act of committing infidelity.

Jacques, who was not yet used to this misfortune and who did not expect it at all, fell ill and the two doctors whom he called diagnosed at first glance an incurable jaundice.

Was it the doctors who got the better of the patient, or the pharmaceuticals? I don't know: the fact remains that he died a fortnight later.

As Jacques had been as good a Catholic as a grocer and, for all the cheeses of the world and of Holland, he would not have joined the Freemasons (like some of his colleagues), his soul, once freed from the carnal rag, went immediately to sit at the feet of the Lord—if a soul can sit!

When God deigned to notice him, he first smiled at Jacques, after which he spoke to him roughly in the following terms. I say roughly because telephone communications between paradise and our little globe are currently in a rudimentary state. But the Financial Companies have such a broad scale that the day is not far off when one of them will announce the exploitation of the Milky Way with the establishment of a telephone line: Capital Unlimited.

So, I return to the words of the Eternal Father, which were more or less:

"From what I have seen, my brave Jacques—and you know that I see everything—I understand that you have not been the happiest one in your household. However, as unfaithful women will soon be as numerous as the stars of the sky and the grains of sand, I am becoming alarmed and have resolved to punish them. In truth, a few years ago I deemed it necessary to remove a rib from Adam to create the first woman, but I have always said the daughters of Eve should at least recognize it. So, my brave Jacques, instead of opening the twin doors of Paradise to you, I am going to send you back to earth to avenge your fellow men.

The soul of Jacques, very happy to be have been chosen by God for such a mission, passed without a murmur into the body of a magnificent macaw.

Why a macaw? The designs of Providence are always obscure . . . like those of some painters!

II

MME PÉTROMÉ, the widow, mourned her dead husband a little more than she had loved him (that is to say, so she would not catch the world's attention) and, when the year of mourning was over, she married the man whom she had already chosen during her husband's lifetime.

It is a singular thing that married men believe they must abandon the gallant and distinguished manners which they exercised when they were lovers, and so immediately resume their coarse, heavy but (shall I say it?) natural manners. Those alone who have enough wit to remain lovers, although legitimately married, can be assured of the fidelity of their wives. But how many are so thoughtful?

Admittedly, Marguerite's new husband was not among these beautiful exceptions.

Once married it was not long before he became sullen, sour and much more virtuous than before. However, as with all good things, virtue may be somewhat useful but it should not be abused, especially in marriage.

Marguerite was doubtless of this opinion, for she deceived her second husband like the first, except that she took precautions against danger.

But, alas! It was the design of the Lord to punish the overly fickle wife, and this is how Providence carried out his design.

A few weeks after her marriage, Marguerite's new husband bought a parrot to which he gave the name of Jacquot and which—the reader has guessed it—contained the soul of Jacques Pétromé.

Jacquot, perched on his perch in the living room, attended all the meeting of the two lovers, and had ended up remembering this sentence always repeated by Marguerite to her lover:

"You can enter, Georges, my foolish husband is away!"

How he raged, that poor parrot!

One day, the lover did not come to the meeting. Chance—which doesn't make mistakes—had the husband come in his place. The husband, being an honest husband, was chatting with his wife and pressing her gently like an unhurried man when Jacquot, not hearing his mistress pronounce the sacramental sentence, did as the prompter at the theater does when the actors hesitate: he voiced the sentence, and so clearly that the husband heard it very well and understood it even better.

Marguerite had only time to feign fainting; fainting being the best response of women. The poor husband had nothing more to learn—he knew everything.

Master Jacquot was happy, but his happiness did not last long, as the husband, seeking to inflict his anger after having broken some pieces of furniture, took the poor bird by the skin of its neck and squeezed so tightly that he suddenly strangled Jacquot.

As it was, the soul of Jacques Pétromé did not regret having to leave the body of the parrot. For, arriving the second time at the feet of the Lord, the latter opened Paradise to him, where he never met his wife again. You may see that complete happiness comes, sooner or later.

For those who can read between the lines, this tale, which is much lighter than what my telling of it may earn me, proves several things, namely:

That the Lord watches over our little globe.

That Virtue is rewarded, eventually.

That my prose has more of that than it has sense.

Finally, everything is for the best in the best of Heavens, where I wish you, dear readers, to go as far from now as is possible.

THE CRUCIAL GRIN

(originally published as "La Grimace Décisive"
in *Le Journal Pour Tous*, August 12, 1898)

I

HE was at her feet, kneeling, ecstatic, and looking up, a silent prayer in his love-moistened eyes, while with his lips he covered her hand with kisses, her hand which had nonchalantly abandoned him.

"Come," she said, suddenly giving to her face a serious expression, almost severe, "you are just a child, René. I was able, in a moment of madness, to let you whisper vague words of love and not to withdraw my hand when you pressed it longer than was necessary; not to be angry when, sitting together on the rustic bench of the garden, your arm slid gently from my shoulder to my waist; and I received with pleasure the kiss you gave me on leaving, as to a mother. Yes, I was able to lend myself to these fantasies without fear, for you were so young! But I must not continue these dangerous games, because they could be fatal to us both!"

"Do not talk so, you make me suffer too much! You know very well that I love you. Why do you not love me?"

"Poor child! You are scarcely twenty, and I am nearly thirty. I am far too old for you. Go love a young girl, ignorant of life, who will offer you the flower of her youth in bloom in exchange for your love."

"If you only have this reason to give me, I do not accept it because it is worthless. I do not care if you are thirty or twenty years old, since I love you! I know only one thing, that you are beautiful, more beautiful than the youngest of the most beautiful. When your eyes meet mine, a delicious weakness invades my whole body, and I have only one desire, that of tightening you against my heart for a long time, even if it meant dying in that embrace."

"Be quiet, my friend, you speak foolishness. You forget that I am not available. What would my husband say if he saw you at this moment, at my feet in this boudoir? Have you not," she added, with an adorable pout in which a smile grinned, "benefited from the lessons of philosophy which he gave you when you attended his class?"

"Not only happy to make me suffer, now you laugh at me. But beware, I am no longer a schoolboy and if it took my fancy I could squeeze this hand that I kiss, strongly enough to make you scream."

René scratched furiously with his nails, at the silk of the cushion on which he had knelt. She, very moved to find so much willpower in this child with the frail looks of a woman, resumed:

"And your mother, who is one of my best friends, what would she say if she knew that not only have I let her son talk to me about love, but that I listened to him with complacency?"

"Why these assumptions? Who else but you could tell my mother that I love you madly? You know very well that if I were loved in return, I would be too jealous of my happiness not to keep that the deepest secret!"

"Decidedly, you are a problem child, much more trouble than a man. Nothing can convince you."

But he, too inexperienced in love to know that the moment when women pile up the difficulties and discuss them is the moment that precedes their abandonment, resumed with despair:

"You do not love me and I am very sad! You played with me as with a child, without realizing that this child might have as much passion as a man. Why have you looked at me so many times, with those eyes full of languor, if you do not want me to love you? Why do you smile at me, as you still do at this moment, if you will prevent me from closing your lips with kisses?"

"You speak like a child! There are other women whose looks are full of languor and whose smile calls the kiss to the lips. Stop your visits for a few days and you will see that soon you will not even think of me again, and when you have forgotten me you will not be far from loving another. You are of the age when the Soul, swollen by a powerful sap of love, flourishes in a thousand passions. You love me today, you say. Will you love me tomorrow?"

"You blaspheme! Be quiet, please! I love you, I will always love you, for there is no look that troubles me as yours does, and no smiling woman made me as thirsty for kisses as you have. It is impossible for me not to see you every day, since every night I dream of you. If love, like an overflow of sap, floods from my soul, it is you who are the cause, you alone, do you hear me? What is the good of bringing your husband up between us? Older than you by so many years, entirely devoted to science, he is a cold philosopher who does not know how to love you, as I would like to love you, with all the ardor of my nature. What is your answer now?"

But, pleasantly surprised to discover in this imperious child a love and a passion so masculine, she rose from the divan on which she lay and said, showing the portrait of her husband enshrined in a blue plush frame:

"You do not think, my friend that I love my husband?"

"Well! This is for him . . ."

Approaching the portrait and despite his jealousy, René flashed an adorable grin from which, between his two white rows of teeth, rose the pink tip of his tongue.

So, instead of smiling or getting angry, she remained very dreamy. And, suddenly seizing the big child who was standing beside her ashamed of his lack of respect, ready to ask for forgiveness, she embraced him with her arms and put on his lips the first kiss of love.

❋

Why is it necessary that, at the most delicious moments of our existence, weird thoughts that come we know not how take possession of our minds to the point of disturbing the present delights? Our brains, so incomprehensible in the mysterious work of thought, take pleasure in these evocations, as abrupt as they are importunate.

While replying to the kisses of his mistress, René was suddenly overwhelmed by one of these fatal visions. He thought perhaps, at the moment when he was enjoying the sweets of adultery, that fruit is all the more pleasing when it is forbidden fruit! The husband, a grave philosopher, had dissembled from his pulpit on the conjugal virtue of Penelope in the fable and on the heroism of Lucretia in history and so, despite himself, a smile came to his pursed lips.

"Why are you laughing, René?

But he, not wishing to evoke the shades of antiquity, pointed to the frame with the portrait of the husband, and replied:

"I think it will be necessary to replace that pale blue plush with a one of golden yellow."

"Naughty, will you be quiet? If he heard us . . ."

And, with a new kiss, she closed his lips.

A PARTIAL LIST OF SNUGGLY BOOKS

Printed in the USA
CPSIA information can be obtained
at www.ICGtesting.com
LVHW040353220124
769411LV00104B/1100